MR. BERNARD'S SAINT BERNARD

Written by *Walter A. Bernard*
Illustrated by *Lauren Scott*

Published in the United States of America
First edition 2015

BZ Books
Wexford, PA 15090
bzbookss@gmail.com

ISBN: 978-0692-46436-6
EISBN: 978-0-692-46437-3

Illustrations by Lauren Scott
Cover Design by Pixel Studios
Interior Design by Ashton Designs

Dedicated to my father, Mr. Bernard and his loving dog, Bernard. May they both rest in peace.

Thank you for showing the world that those who are pure in heart are blessed.

–Walter A. Bernard

One rainy day, Mr. Bernard heard a knock at his door.

Mr. Bernard opened the door and found a big brown box on his doorstep.

He looked around to see who dropped off the box, but no one was there.

Mr. Bernard heard a loud noise coming from inside the box.

"I wonder what that noise could be," he said.

Mr. Bernard pressed his ear against the box to see if he could hear anything.

The top of the box popped off in the air and a fluffy Saint Bernard puppy jumped out of the box and onto the ground.

The excited puppy had a red collar with a golden name tag that read, "Bernie."

Mr. Bernard smiled at the puppy and asked, "If I take care of you today, will you take care of me tomorrow?"

Bernie jumped up on Mr. Bernard's leg.

"I guess that means yes," Mr. Bernard giggled.

Bernie was stinky and his fur was very dirty.

"You need a bath, Bernie," said Mr. Bernard.

So he picked Bernie up and put him in the bathtub which was full of warm water.

4

Bernie had never had a bath before and was frightened of the water.

"Don't be afraid Bernie," laughed Mr. Bernard. "It's only soap and water."

"If I clean you today, will you clean me tomorrow?"

Bernie grinned from ear to ear because he knew that Mr. Bernard was there to protect him.

Bernie began splashing the water in the tub and got Mr. Bernard all wet.

He washed Bernie until Bernie was all cleaned up. Next, Mr. Bernard took Bernie out of the bathtub and rubbed him with a towel until he was dry and all fluffy.

"Now, time to brush your teeth, Bernie," said Mr. Bernard

Mr. Bernard wanted to brush Bernie's teeth so he wouldn't get cavities.

Over time, Mr. Bernard and Bernie became best friends.

One day, Mr. Bernard woke up early and put on his blue overalls so he could work in the backyard with Bernie.

He looked at Bernie and said, "If we take care of the tree today, it will take care of us tomorrow."

They spent all morning planting a beautiful lemon tree.

Bernie helped dig a deep hole. Next, Mr. Bernard planted the tree into the hole.

Throughout the rest of the year, Mr. Bernard and Bernie went to the backyard and watered the lemon tree using the water hose. The lemon tree grew and grew until it started making lemons.

After Mr. Bernard watered the tree, he took the water hose and let Bernie drink from it.

"If I give you water today, will you give me water tomorrow?"

Bernie responded with a "Ruff!" as water dripped from his drooling mouth.

When Mr. Bernard had to get up in the morning for work, he didn't have to use an alarm clock because Bernie nibbled on his toes to wake him up.

"Woof, woof!" roared Bernie. Then Mr. Bernard knew it was time to get up.

When Mr. Bernard left for work, Bernie would lay on the grass underneath the lemon tree waiting for Mr. Bernard to come home.

As Bernie lay under the lemon tree he watched the blue jays chirp, the squirrels chase each other, and the beautiful butterflies flutter their wings.

Every once in a while a ripe,
yellow lemon would fall from
the lemon tree.

Bernie picked up the lemons
and put them in a pile for Mr.
Bernard.

When Mr. Bernard arrived home, Bernie ran as fast as he could towards Mr. Bernard, wagging his tail with excitement.

"You missed me today, will you miss me tomorrow?" Mr. Bernard joked with Bernie.

Mr. Bernard took all of the lemons from Bernie's pile and made lemonade for the whole neighborhood.

All of the boys and girls came over to his yard to drink lemonade.

"We took care of the tree yesterday and now it's taking care of us today," Mr. Bernard said while sipping his lemonade in the hot sun.

"Mr. Bernard, we want to play catch with Bernie! Can we play catch with him today?" the children yelled.

Catch was Bernie's favorite game.

"If you play catch with him today, will you play catch with him tomorrow?" asked Mr. Bernard.

"Yes!" the children replied. "We want to play catch with Bernie every day!"

The fastest girl in the neighborhood grabbed the green ball and threw it as far as she could. Whoosh.

Bernie chased the ball down and ran as fast as his long legs could take him.

Bernie played with the children until the sun went down. It was nearly Bernie's bedtime.

Mr. Bernard brushed Bernie's coat and told him what a great friend he was.

Bernie liked to get his hair brushed before he went to bed.

The next morning, Bernie sat at the foot of Mr. Bernard's bed holding his leash in his mouth.

"Oh Bernie, what is it now?"

Bernie waited for Mr. Bernard to get up as he wagged his tail back and forth.

Mr. Bernard looked at Bernie and said, "If I walk you today, will you walk me tomorrow?"

Bernie let out a, "Ruff!"

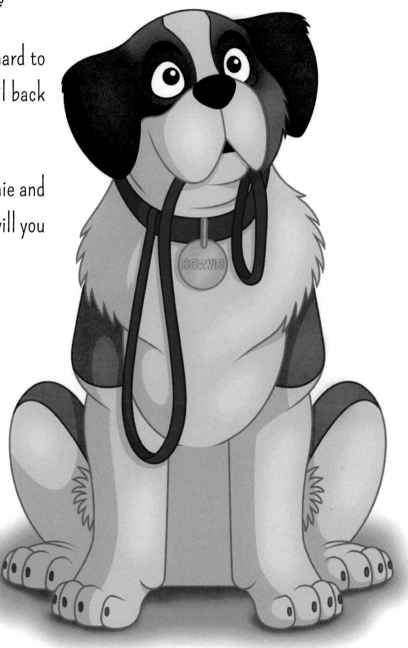

Mr. Bernard put on his shoes and took Bernie out for a walk through the neighborhood.

The kids recognized Bernie and shouted his name as he walked by, "Hi Bernie!"

For many years, Mr. Bernard walked Bernie and always asked him, "If I walk you today, will you walk me tomorrow?"

As time went on, Mr. Bernard grew old and his eyesight grew weak. He needed glasses but could not afford to buy a pair. He spent all of his life giving to others.

It soon became difficult for him to walk so he used a wheel chair to get around.

The children in the neighborhood had grown up and were now getting ready to start college.

One day Mr. Bernard, sat in his wheelchair and, in a soft voice, he called out, "Bernie!"

Wagging his tail, Bernie slowly walked over to Mr. Bernard.

"Bernie... I am tired and I am weak. I am an old man now. Yesterday is gone and tomorrow is finally here. I can no longer walk you anymore. Will you walk me today?"

23

Bernie let out a gentle "Ruff!" and handed Mr. Bernard the red leash. Mr. Bernard held onto the leash and this time, Bernie took Mr. Bernard for a walk around the neighborhood.

Mr. Bernard smiled because he saw the kids that used to come by his house to play catch with Bernie. Even though they were all grown up, in Mr. Bernard's eyes, they were still the kids who loved his lemonade and enjoyed playing with Bernie.

When Bernie and Mr. Bernard arrived home, there was a big red box at the doorstep.

"I wonder what's in the box," Mr. Bernard questioned.

Bernie opened the box for Mr. Bernard.

Inside the box was a brand new pair of glasses for Mr. Bernard. There was a note inside from the neighborhood kids that read;

"You took care of us yesterday,
so we will take care of you today,
tomorrow and forever."

The End